THE EASY-TO-READ
LITTLE ENGINE
THAT COULD

A Platt & Munk **ALL ABOARD BOOK**™

THE EASY-TO-READ LITTLE ENGI

Platt & Munk, Publishers

Copyright © 1986, 1957, 1930 by Platt & Munk, Publishers, a division of Grosset & Dunlap, Inc., which is a member of The Putnam Publishing Group, New York. All rights reserved. THE LITTLE ENGINE THAT COULD, engine design, and "I THINK I CAN" are trademarks of Platt & Munk, Publishers. ALL ABOARD BOOKS is a trademark of The Putnam Publishing Group. Published simultaneously in Canada. Printed in the U.S.A. Library of Congress Catalog Card Number: 86-80291 ISBN 0-448-19078-8

1992 Printing

AT COULD

By Watty Piper

Adapted for young readers by Walter Retan

Illustrated by Mateu

Chug chug chug. Puff puff puff.
The little train ran along the tracks.
She was a happy little train. Her cars
were full of good things for boys and girls.

There were all kinds of toy animals.

Giraffes with long necks,

teddy bears
with no necks,

and even a baby
elephant.

here were all kinds of dolls.

Dolls with blue eyes
and yellow hair,

dolls with brown eyes
and brown hair,

and the funniest toy clown
you ever saw.

There were toy trucks, airplanes, and boats.
There were picture books, games, and drums to play.
The little train carried every kind of toy that
boys or girls could want.

But that was not all. The little train carried good things to eat, too.

Big, round oranges…

fat, red apples…

long, yellow bananas…

fresh, cold milk…

and lollipops to eat after dinner.

The little train was taking all these good things
to the other side of the mountain.

"How happy the boys and girls will be to see me!"
said the little train. "They will like the toys and good food
that I am bringing."

But all at once the train came to a stop.
he did not move at all.
  "Oh, dear," said the little train. "What can be the matter?"
She tried to start up again. She tried and tried.
ut her wheels just would not turn.

"We can help," said the toy animals.

The clown and the animals climbed out of their cars.

They tried to push the little train.

But she did not move.

"We can help, too," said the dolls. And they got out and tried to push.
Still the little train did not move.
The toys and dolls did not know what to do.

Just then a shiny new engine came puffing down another track.

"Maybe that engine can help us!" cried the clown

He began to wave a red flag. The Shiny New Engine slowed down.

he dolls and toys called out to him. "Our engine
t working," they said. "Please pull our train over
mountain. If you do not, the boys and girls will
ave any toys or good food."

The Shiny New Engine was not friendly.
"You want *me* to pull *you*?" he asked. "That is not what I do. I carry people. They sit in cars with soft seats. They look out big windows. They eat in a nice dining car. They can even sleep in a fine sleeping car.

"*I* pull the likes of you? I should say not!"
Off went the Shiny New Engine without another word.

How sad all the toys and dolls felt!

Then the toy clown called out, "Here comes another engine. A big, strong one. Maybe *this* engine will help us."

Again the clown waved his flag. The Big Strong Engine came to a stop.

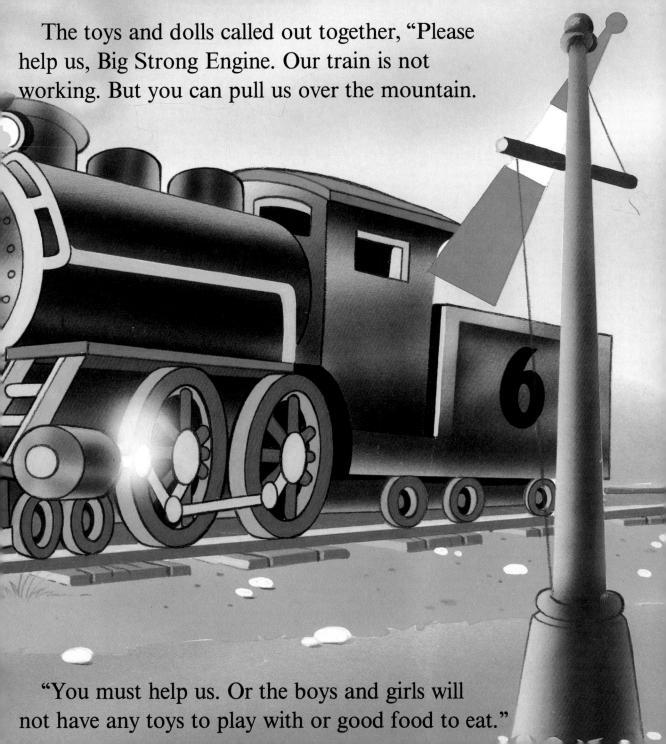

The toys and dolls called out together, "Please help us, Big Strong Engine. Our train is not working. But you can pull us over the mountain.

"You must help us. Or the boys and girls will not have any toys to play with or good food to eat."

But the Big Strong Engine did not want to help.
"I do not pull toys," he said. "I pull cars
full of heavy logs. I pull big trucks. I have no
time for the likes of you."

And away puffed the Big Strong Engine
without another word.

y this time the little train was no longer
ppy train.
nd the dolls and toys were ready to cry.
ut the clown called out, "Look! Look!
ther engine is coming. A little blue engine.
ry little one. Maybe *this* engine
help us."

The Little Blue Engine was a happy engine.
She saw the clown waving his red flag
and stopped at once.

"What is the matter?" she asked in a kind way.

"Oh, Little Blue Engine," cried the dolls
and toys. "Will you pull us over the mountain?
Our engine is not working. If you do not help,
the boys and girls will have no toys or good food.
"Just over the mountain.
"Please, please help us."

"Oh, my," said the Little Blue Engine. "I am not very big. And I do not pull trains. I just work in the yards. I have never even been over the mountain."

"But we *must* get there before the children wake up," said the toys and dolls. "Please?"

The Little Blue Engine looked at the dolls and toys. She could see that they were not happy.

She thought about the children on the other side of the mountain. Without toys or good food, they would not be happy either.

The Little Blue Engine pulled up close.
She took hold of the little train.
The toys and dolls climbed back into their cars.

At last the Little Blue Engine said,
"I think I can climb up the mountain.
I think I can. I think I can."

Then the Little Blue Engine began to pull.
She tugged and she pulled. She pulled
and she tugged.

Puff puff, *chug chug* went the little engine.
"I think I can. I think I can," she said.
Slowly, slowly, the train started to move.
The dolls and toys began to smile and clap.

Puff puff, chug chug.

Up the mountain went the Little Blue Engine.

And all the time she kept saying, "I think
I can, I think I can, I think I can...."

Up, up, up. The little engine climbed
and climbed.

At last she reached the top of the mountain.
Down below lay the city.

"Hurray! Hurray!" cried the dolls and animals.

"The boys and girls will be so happy,"
said the toy clown. "All because you helped us,
Little Blue Engine."

The Little Blue Engine just smiled.

But as she puffed down the mountain,
the Little Blue Engine seemed to say...
"I thought I could. I thought I could.
I thought I could. I thought I could."